THE DEVIL IN THE WOODS

JESSACA WILLIS

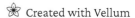 Created with Vellum

MORE BOOKS BY JESSACA WILLIS

THE CURSED KINGDOMS OF GRIMTOL

A Delicate Betrayal, Book 0

TBA

REAPERS OF VELTUUR

Assassin Reaper, Book 0

Soul of the Crow, Book 1

Heart of the Sungem, Book 2

Fate of the Vulture, Book 3

PRIMORDIALS OF SHADOWTHORN

Shadow Crusade, Book 1

Blighted Heart, Book 2

Immortal Return, Book 3

BLOOD & MAGIC ETERNAL

Hunger & Cursed Shadows, Book 0

Blood & Magic Eternal, Book 1

TBA

THE AWAKENED

The Awakening, Book 0

Blood Awakens, Book 1

Puppets Dream, Book 2

TBA

Be the feral creature you were always destined to be.

CONTENTS

ONE

The Devil has cursed us.

He's plagued the women of our town with madness. Vexed them into oblivion. And I am afraid my dearest Cecily might be next.

Her slender hand is still outstretched, one finger trembling behind the ruffled cuff of her sleeve as she points to the trees across the meadow.

"There," she whispers, her voice as unsettling as the fog that surrounds us. "Do you see it?"

"See what?" I ask, abruptly darting behind the willow tree we had just been tumbling under. If she's right, if someone has been spying on us, then they've already witnessed our most scandalous transgressions, so I'm not sure why I even bother trying to conceal myself. Still, I make haste as I finish tightening the laces of my stay. "Who is it? Who did you see?"

Before I can finish knotting the cord, Cecily tugs me away from the tree and situates me before her.

I should be as worried as she is. If anyone saw us, who knows what they would do. If the Father knew what we had been up to, he would call us worse than deplorable wretches. He might even suggest the town cast us into the woods to rid them of our wickedness.

But pressed up against her like this, with her lily perfume teasing me, reminding me just how decadent the contours of her neck taste upon my tongue, makes my heart thunder for her all over again.

We knew the risks. We knew we could get caught. And yet, I still wouldn't choose differently. Not when our time together is already dwindling.

"Not *who*," she corrects, her grasp on my shoulders tightening. It's only then that I remember there are worse things to be spotted among the trees. Her voice is quivering like one of the few last leaves holding onto the branches before winter. "There. The red eyes. You see them, Ellowyn. Don't you?"

She's beginning to sound like Edith. Like all the others who disappeared this last year. Taken away by the Devil in the woods.

I can't even fathom her suffering a similar fate, but for Cecily's sake—and perhaps for mine—I squint harder and force my gaze upon the dark, looming forest before us. The sun has already begun its descent, casting shadows between the trees that look more like ominous hollows than the patchwork of serene greenery we found ourselves entranced by earlier. My stomach was fluttering then, a swirl of butterflies that wanted to float us into the clouds and never come back down.

Now my stomach churns like it's full of centipedes.

I might not *see* it, but I'd have to be a fool not to notice that the air has gone taut.

We should be getting home soon.

Both of us.

Before someone starts to wonder why we were so far away from town, so close to the woods that we are not meant to be nearing.

Slowly, I shake my head, making the ringlets around my ears tickle my goose-pimpled flesh. "I'm sorry. I don't see a thing."

Cecily releases me so harshly that I'm practically thrown out of her arms.

Mouth agape, I twist around to face her, prepared to demand that she treat me in a gentler manner henceforth, but her horror-stricken features stop me. The curve of her bottom lip quivers, tears already streaking her tawny cheeks as her gaze remains transfixed on the dark forest now behind me.

We both know what this means.

The visions always come first.

And then...

My strides are like cracks of thunder as I storm across the space between us, as if each pounding of my heel can crunch the roots below before they could ever snatch her away, before they could claim her like they had so many others.

I grip her dainty shoulders, feel the warmth of her skin through her chemise. "I will not let anyone take you away from me. Do you understand?"

"You...you mean that?" She looks up at me from lowered lashes and it does strange things to my insides. To my heart. I would give anything to keep her looking at me like that, with so much trust and hope and love—a love that was unbreakable, no matter how much we endured.

Nodding, I tuck a stray hair the color of a raven's feather behind her ear. "Of course I mean it."

"Not even Albert?"

My hands fall from her shoulders and I step back. The harsh cold settles between us. "You know I have no say over that. Your parents have already arranged it."

"But we could leave, you and I. Start a new life, together."

"Leave?" I laugh. "Are you mad? Where would we go? We're just women. We have no money to our names. No property. No trades. We have nowhere else to go."

"Forget it. It was a foolish daydream and should never have been uttered aloud." Cecily huffs, her arms folding around the very waist I had just been kissing moments prior. "Don't worry about me. Within the fortnight, I won't be yours to protect anymore anyway."

It is a cold dagger to the chest. A sharp slice through my heart.

We already agreed not to speak of her betrothal, so I don't know why she is bringing it up—now of all moments.

We only have two weeks left together before Cecily will leave to marry some earl her family adores, while I am left to rot in Thimbleton alone.

I might never see her again.

I might never hold her. Or kiss her.

"Let's not talk about that."

I reach for her honeyed hands to anchor me—to anchor us both, but she steps back, her expression a storm of fury and terror.

"Fine. We won't talk about it. The whole betrothal might be futile now anyway since I might not even make it that long." Throwing her hands out, she gestures to the woods.

"Don't say that!" I reach for her, but she pulls away.

"You know it's true, Ellowyn. Those...those creatures in the forest, they're coming for me. Today proves it."

"Today proves nothing—"

"Does it not?" Cecily's voice pitches like a lark being strangled by a snake, and I can do nothing to ease her fear. "And what about yesterday when I told you I felt eyes upon me all day?"

"We don't know what that was—"

"No, *you* don't know what that was. I do. I know what I felt...what I saw." Her haunted gaze returns to the woods, like she's desperate to see the red eyes again

5

to prove they were there and that she's not losing her mind like all the others.

I want to tell her that we will figure this out together. But as if she can hear the thought, she holds up a hand and silences me before I can find the encouraging words.

"There is nothing you or anyone can do to stop Him, just like there was nothing we could do to save the others."

Cecily is right.

Deep down, I know she is.

Because the townsfolk *did* try.

Last spring when the Viscount's wife, Edith, stumbled into the marketplace, the hem of her skirt sodden, her hair as wild as a robin's nest, we took in her every warning, no matter how frenzied her words. Evil spirits in the forest. Stalking the women. Preying upon any who dare wander near.

We sent our strongest men to search the forest. They found nothing.

One week later, Edith had disappeared for good. Not all of her though. A few children found her face etched into a tree on the outskirts of the forest the same day she went missing. A warning to all of us to keep our distance.

Six more women have been taken since. The men who have ventured after them were left discarded and mangled at the edge of the woods, almost as if the trees themselves had chewed them up and spat them out again.

Not the women though.

The forest seems to like us. It craves us the way the ocean craves the shore. And for each woman that forest has taken, their faces have left their mark on the trees, an ode to the souls it has trapped there.

I will not let that happen to my Cecily.

"I better be going," she says, a bite in her tone that's rarely ever been directed at me. "It's getting dark and it's...it's not safe to be out here."

With her skirts clutched in her hands, she turns her back to me and flees.

I stand there, clenching my fists so that my nails dig bloodied, crescent-shaped moons into the palms of my hands.

When I utter my vow, the blood that drips to the earth makes the promise feel all the more binding:

"No one shall take her from me. Not an earl. Not the forest. Not even the Devil, Himself."

CHAPTER
TWO

S leep evades me all night. The vow I made rumbles through me, awakening something voracious that I didn't even know existed inside me.

It rattles my bones well into the morning until I cannot fight it any longer. I throw the wool blankets to the foot of the bed, my body abuzz as I set out to save the love of my life.

But where do I begin?

No one in town seems to understand what has been occurring in the forest. For over a year, our women have disappeared, and the men have long since stopped chasing after them because all it has brought is more heartbreak. More devastation. So no one knows what happens to the women. No one knows where their bodies go, or why their faces keep appearing in the trees.

However, every Sunday Father Thomas preaches about the darkness that looms over those woods, so I decide to visit him first.

On my way to the church, I pick some fresh cornflowers and daisies, and hold them against my chest so that they might disguise my sinful heart from the Father and from God. Maybe if I play the role of a beautiful maiden, if I mask myself behind a bouquet of purity, perhaps no one will discover me as the lecherous creature I am—or maybe that's the very reason Cecily has been marked. Maybe it's because we had been frolicking in the meadow without a care for who should see us, ignorant to the dangers of drawing the forest's eye.

I clutch the flowers tighter as I enter the church.

Inside, I find Father Thomas sitting diligently in a pew. Quietly, I tiptoe forward, taking a seat behind him to wait until he finishes his prayers, and when he does, he glances over his shoulder to see who has arrived.

I bow my head, staring down at the flowers pressed against my chest, their petals already wilted at the ends. "Hello, Father. Forgive my intrusion."

Father Thomas smiles as I lift my head. "Ah, Ellowyn. You intrude on nothing. It is good to see you." In the candlelit church, his eyes appear darker than usual, like an animal lurking in the night. His gaze wanders down to the flowers pressed against my bosom —or at least, I hope that's where its lingering. "What a sight for sore eyes those are. Sadly, I'm afraid there are no vases in the church to display them."

"Oh, of course. My apologies." My cheeks burst into flames, mirroring the fire that should've consumed me upon entering this sacred space. Maybe he's staring at the flowers because he sees them for what they truly are: an embarrassing rouse that is unlikely fooling anyone. "I just—with all the gloom surrounding Thimbleton of late, I thought..."

The inside of my mouth becomes as dry as cottonwood seeds. I didn't think this conversation through. I thought the words would flow freely, but it's like they're buried inside me—and for good reason. The last two women to come forth about their hallucinations have been isolated from the rest of the town, all in the name of their own safety, of course. I was in full support of the decision when I first heard they were being taken to the doctor's for care—anything to protect our people from being lost to that dreaded forest.

But now I can't help the worry twisting around in my gut.

If I bring up Cecily, if I tell him about what she claims to have seen, Father Thomas will have her taken away. He might do the same to me just for associating with her.

The church feels heavier with shadows today. Like no amount of candlelight can shine through the darkness that hangs from the steeple as thick as moss. I can't keep my eyes from wandering up there, searching for the evil that I fear is closing in around this town.

"Are you alright, Ellowyn?" he asks, drawing me from my mental spiraling. "You look pale."

It's no wonder, I can hardly find air. My corset feels as if it is tightening around my waistline, the stiff panels squeezing the life out of me.

But I need to concoct a lie and fast. One that won't rouse his suspicions about my dearest Cecily or myself.

"I—I have just been so worried lately, Father."

His thick brows pinch. "Worried? About what, my child?" When I don't immediately reply, he drags his hands down the front of his black cassock before patiently folding his hands in his lap. "This is safe place. God is watching over you."

That was always part of the problem, though, wasn't it? Part of the reason why my palms sweat every time I step foot under this roof. Every time I pray at the edge of my bed.

If God is watching over me, if he saw every secret glance I shared with Cecily and had witnessed our flesh becoming one on more occasions than I can count anymore, then the two of us are condemned already.

Being taken by the forest would be the least of our problems.

I swallow the hot lump in my throat.

"Well, yes, Father. But it's not me who I'm worried about. It's the girls. The ones who said—" I cup a hand around my mouth and whisper conspiratorially "—the ones who said they saw evil spirits in the forest."

The Father doesn't even flinch.

I am likely not the first woman to come to him with such fears.

He reaches to pat my shoulder, and I shudder against the chilling caress of his fingers even through my bodice. "There, there, Ellowyn. You mustn't worry your simple mind with such things. Catherine and Beatrice are in good hands. Doctor Egerton is overseeing their care now, and he is doing a fine job of keeping both of those young woman safe and far out of the reaches of the wickedness plaguing them. In fact, I hear he and Catherine just announced an engagement."

The news is so shocking, so unexpected, that I don't even know how to react at first. "An...engagement?"

His crumpled features make it seem as though he had expected more excitement from me upon hearing the news. But Doctor Egerton is twice Catherine's age— maybe thrice. I'm not even sure they had met prior to her recent episode, which means they've only known each other for a short time. And already they're engaged?

"Yes, an engagement. Don't look so dismayed." His hand snakes up to cup my cheek and I freeze like a deer cornered by a mountain lion. "This is a good thing, Ellowyn. Catherine could use a husband to tend to. It will be good for her recovery to have something to focus on."

Smiling, I use my agreeable nodding to disguise me pulling my face out of his hand, but deep down I couldn't disagree more. As if being a wife was the only worthy hobby to preoccupy her. I know Catherine. She has plenty of hobbies and interests of her own. But surviving in a man's world is all about knowing when to hold your tongue and smile, lest I find myself locked up and betrothed just like her. Like Cecily is soon to be...

"That is wonderful news, Father," I say, and because I want to keep him talking and to tell me something useful, I lay on the flattery as well. "You both are taking such good care of them—of all of us. It's just...I don't want to lose anyone else. And I wish I could help somehow, the way that you do."

His smile is as slippery as a worm. "You can help, my dear. You can pray."

My pleasantness nearly falters, but I manage to maintain the demure, good-girl smile.

Behind my brittle façade though, I want to scream.

Praying has done nothing for us. Edith was a faithful, God-fearing woman. Catherine and Beatrice were as well; so were all the others before them. None of them ever missed a day of church. They were kind neighbors, selfless wives, and patient mothers and sisters. They did everything correctly, obeyed God without fail, and yet they were still punished; they were still taken from us.

I wonder, if it were men being targeted, would our leaders choose a different path? Would they be so passive as one-by-one they all slipped away, never to be heard from or seen again? Or is this just a convenient way of keeping us all in line?

Prayers didn't save Edith. They weren't saving Beatrice or Catherine now. And they most certainly won't save Cecily.

But perhaps I can.

First, I need to know more about the women having these visions. I need to know everything the Father knows.

Tucking one of my ringlets behind my ear, I lower my gaze to my hands and become the virtuous flower I've been raised to be.

"Father, I wonder—it would ease my worries immensely if you could perhaps tell me what part of the forest the Devil seems to be lurking in the most? As you know, my family and I live along its edge, and I only want for us to remain safe."

"As I have said in my sermons, it is best to stay far away from that forest in its entirety."

With his voice as taut as a bowstring, he sounds more like he's evading the question than giving me an actual response. I can't help but push a little harder.

"Yes, of course, Father. But if there were a specific part of the woods where the attacks were happening more regularly, it would be helpful to—"

"What part of avoid the forest at all costs is difficult to comprehend!" Spit spews from his lips as the geyser of unfettered frustration spills from him. His harshness makes me jerk away, my spine banging against the back of the pew and surely leaving a bruise. This is the problem with men who smile through thin lips; their composure is always a hairpin away from fracturing. But he realizes his loss of control almost instantly, and with a long sigh, the Father steels his composure with another smoothing down of his cassock. "Forgive me. It has been a long few weeks and your curiosities about the woods are worrying. Please, Ellowyn, do not go near those woods. As long as you remain in the confines of your own home, you should be safe. None of the attacks have happened indoors. So do not so much as allow yourself to be cast in the trees' shadows, or glance in their direction. For your own safety. Do I make myself clear?"

It's nothing I didn't already know, but I'm not foolish enough to press him again.

Nodding, I force myself to meet his penetrating eyes. "Of course. Thank you, Father. The Devil shall not find me to be so foolish as to wander near his den of vipers."

The crook of his mouth slithers upward with relief. "That's a good girl. Now, run along. And leave the plague of evil surrounding that place for the men to handle."

I flee his presence with no more than a hasty farewell. I used to think it was my own guilty conscious that made me uneasy around him, but not today. Today, the Father did that all on his own—the lingering glances, the unwanted caresses. I welcome the fresh air as I exit the church, and wish I could seek out a warm bath to scrub my skin.

Of course, I don't have time for that.

If the Father isn't going to help me, then I need a new plan.

With Catherine and Beatrice locked away with Doctor Egerton, I can't speak to either of them without rousing suspicions. It leaves me with only one option:

Cecily.

THREE

W hile walking over to Cecily's, I stare at the flowers and vacillate between whether I should toss them to the ground or gift them to her as a peace offering. Both options feel ridiculous. On the one hand, why would I discard a perfectly beautiful bouquet when I could instead deliver it to a perfectly beautiful woman? On the other, I fear the overly simplified yet romantic gesture might make it seem like I think an argument about something as serious as her hallucinations could be fixed by a meager floral arrangement.

By the time I reach her front doorstep, I still haven't decided.

My fist aims at the mahogany door, but freezes before knocking. Over our last decade of friendship— and the half year we've spent as something more— we've had our fair share of quarrels and spats, but nothing like last night. Neither of us have ever left in the middle of an argument like that.

But I'm not prepared to leave it like that forever.

My knuckles ache to the rap-tap-tap tune of my knocking, and as I wait for her to answer, I imagine what she'll say.

"Who brings dead flowers as an apology?"

A small smile tugs at the corner of my lips because I know she'd say it with a smirk as well. We can never stay mad at each other for too long, especially not with her betrothal coming so soon.

But after a few minutes have passed and Cecily still hasn't answered the door, my smile fades from my lips.

It is still rather early in the morning, early enough that I know Cecily hasn't left to start her day yet—today, she and her mother will be visiting the seamstress to fit her for her wedding gown, but that won't be for another few hours at best.

My knock is firmer the second time around, more urgent.

"Cecily!" I call out.

When there is no response still, I toss the flowers to the ground to free my hands so that they can hoist my skirts as I climb upon the cobblestone flower bed to peer into the window.

The house is silent. It is too late for her to still be sleeping. She must still be upset and deliberately ignoring me then.

"Don't pretend you can't hear me! I know you're in

there. The seamstress isn't open yet—I walked by there this morning. So if you're trying to pretend like you're not here, well your rouse is over. So come out here and speak to me, whether you're upset or not, because let me tell you, Cecily McDermot, I am not going anywhere until I—"

The doorknob twists. The thick oak door pulls back with a groan. Cecily's sleepy mother scowls at me from the doorway.

"Mrs. McDermot!" I hop down from the flowerbed and smooth my skirts with the palms of my sweaty hands before greeting her more properly. "My apologies for the ruckus. I just came by to speak with Cecily. Is she still asleep?"

Her mother is a near spitting-image of her, except her hair is the color of smoke twisting up from a dosed flame.

Mrs. McDermot looks up and over her shoulder at the mountain-of-a-man who steps in behind her—Cecily's father. He rests one hand upon his wife's shoulder, but the concerned look they exchange twists my insides.

"What do you mean is she still asleep?" his baritone voice rumbles. "She never came home last night."

"W-we thought she might still be with you?" The hopeful inflection in Mrs. McDermot's voice is like a fractured piece of glass, and I'm about to break it.

"I haven't seen her since sundown," I tell them. "Not since she said she saw something in the woods..."

The hopeful glimmer in her deep brown eyes fades and her hand inches up to clutch onto her husband's. A horrific understanding flashes between them both. Between us all.

My dearest Cecily never made it home last night. And given her recent hallucinations, it can only mean one thing.

The forest has taken her.

I am too late to stop it.

FOUR

TWO WEEKS LATER

T he rain murmurs of melancholy as I sit beneath our willow tree, a new droplet kissing the tip of my nose or brushing past my eyelashes every few seconds.

Oh, how Cecily loved listening to the rain. Nothing was more exciting to her than being caught in a storm. During the last downpour, she chased me to the stables and pulled me under their shelter where she showered me with kisses until I was nothing more than a puddle of ecstasy beneath her touch.

Tears blur with the raindrops. We won't ever share another kiss again.

Every morning, I come here and sit to watch the forest. It makes me feel closer to her, like she is still with me somehow, even though I know she is gone. But it also gives me hope that I might spy her, that she might still be out there trying to make her way back to me and out of the Devil's clutches.

Both her parents and mine worry that I'm spending too much time out here, tempting the Devil to claim me next.

Honestly, I'm not sure that would be all too terrible.

What if He saw me?

What if He chose me?

At least then I would be reunited with the love of my life instead of being left here to rot.

The gloom of the day tries to dissuade me from my post, the downpour around me all but insisting I give up and return home sodden and empty-handed once more.

It's days like these, days so miserable and lonely that I consider darting into the forest without hearing the Devil's call, but I know better. I know not to heed the delirium and desperation filling me like dark ink. The men behaved in such an irrational manner, they raced after Edith and the others, and the forest spewed them out like toxic bile. I might not fully comprehend the supernatural elements at play here, but I know this: the Devil is selective, and only those he invites may enter his cursed lair.

And so I wait.

Each day I return to our willow tree to watch the very place in the woods where Cecily saw the red eyes that still never appear to me.

Today is no different. The only sounds I hear are the raindrops bouncing against the leaves.

At dusk, I begin to collect myself from the soaked earth, when something catches the corner of my eye.

A flash of red. A smear of crimson against the gloomy green forest.

I blink, returning my gaze to the woods. But by the time I'm focused on the bouncing branches again, it's already gone.

If it hadn't been for Cecily proclaiming she saw red eyes watching her from this very spot, I might have ignored it. It came and went so quickly it would have been easy to rationalize as a mere trick of the sun's fading light, or grief finally getting the best of me.

But this was no trick. It *was* there. I saw...something. And even if I hadn't, I can feel it in the air all the same.

Something is watching me.

Something malignant and potent.

The hairs on my arms are as stiff as needles. I square my shoulders, heart pounding in my chest as I meet the forest's dark gaze.

"Hello? Is...anyone there?"

The rain is all that answers.

Over the torrential downpour, it would be impossible to hear anything, so I venture a cautious step closer, one that I hope won't be my ruin.

Still, there is nothing out of the ordinary. No more splash of red. No voices speaking to me.

I inch closer. And closer. Until I am right up against the dark forest's edge, so close that I can reach out and drag a finger along one of the slick leaves, if I so dare.

There is a sharpness in my chest that steals my breath away. It forces my voice into a shaky whisper. "Cecily, are you there?"

Branches jostle beneath the weight of the rain. I wait and watch with hope brimming in my chest, but it is not Cecily, nor anything from within the woods that calls to me.

"Ellowyn! What in God's name are you doing?"

A man's voice, harsh and reprimanding, jerks me from the woods. I snap around to find Father Thomas marching toward me, watching me with such reproach that I feel like a small child beneath his gaze.

"F-father Thomas!" With one hand shielding my face, I jog to meet him beneath what little cover the willow tree can provide. Despite my best efforts, I'm still drenched and practically drowning as I ask, "What are you doing out here?"

He scoffs, those beady eyes of his dragging down the length of me and back up again. Suddenly, I find myself wishing I had worn more layers, or thicker ones that weren't sticking to every contour of my body.

"I might ask you the same," he said. "From the looks of it, you were mere seconds away from entering those damned woods." I shake my head in protest, but he will hear none of it. "Don't deny it. I saw you talking to someone."

Suddenly, the intensity in his eyes takes on a new meaning. No longer does he seem like a man riddled with worry for my well-being, nor like someone who came all this way with the intention of merely checking on me and my poor forlorn heart.

There's a darkness in his gaze, a wildness to the set of his eyes that makes my stomach churn.

We are alone. Whatever happens here, it will be his word against mine, and in my grief these past weeks, my waning sanity has already been the town's gossip. If I am not careful with my response, I could be labelled a madwoman just like all the others.

"I—I wasn't speaking to anyone, Father. I swear it."

My voice is so quiet it can hardly be heard over the rain, but I don't want to risk the volume of it making me appear like I've already lost my mind. Like I'm more brazen or crazed than I should be. I am not one of the women they found in hysterics. I am not haunted—or at least my sanity has not yet been compromised, and I will not have him thinking otherwise.

He still looks unconvinced, so I dip my head to hide the shame in my eyes as I mutter, "I was calling her name, in case she can still hear me."

I had expected the confession to cool him. But somehow it has the opposite effect.

Father Thomas widens his stance, pinning me between him and the deadly forest as if my only options are to face his judgment or be fed to the evil in the woods.

His teeth flash, clamped like fangs. "You're trying to commune with—with one of the Devil's harlots?"

"What? No! Father, Cecily isn't one of—"

"The Cecily you knew is gone, Ellowyn!" Father Thomas takes a step closer, and it takes everything within me not to shrink away from his imposing stature. He's not even a large man, but he moves like a noxious gas, filling the space between us in the blink of an eye. "The Devil coaxed her with His falsities and wicked promises, and her mind was weak, so she obliged Him. She went to Him. She followed the Devil into His den and now there is no saving her. There is no saving any of them."

My lip warbles, but I am rendered speechless.

It cannot be true.

Cecily is not gone.

She can't be.

Cecily is not weak-minded. She is the fiercest person I know. She is the last ember left burning after the fire has been doused. She is a sapling sprouting from a downed tree after a woodsman has chopped it to pieces. She is unwavering and loyal and devout, and she is nothing like the pitiful, flinching creature he has painted her to be.

Of course, I can tell him none of it. The tightness in his jaw and the way his eyes watch me like a fox stalking prey are a warning that I shall heed. Any attempt at denial or defense will only condemn me.

"There is no saving any of the women who have wandered from God's path," he continues, gentler now that I am not arguing. But his words are still configured like traps waiting to snap their jaws around me, should I falter. "I thought you of all people understood that."

"Of course, Father. Forgive me." I pretend the wetness on my face is as much from the rain as it is from my tears, and I wipe the pain away. "My grief is getting the better of me."

"Indeed it is," he says, patting my shoulder. "I know you miss your friend, but it is not safe for you to remain out here alone. I fear the effects this isolation is having on your mental state, not to mention the danger you're putting yourself in daily."

I nod, hoping it will put an end to the conversation sooner so that I can resume searching for the red eyes that I think might have appeared to me.

But Father Thomas' tone softens again, his thumb stroking my collarbone in small circles that twist my stomach in knots.

"In fact, it's why I spoke to your parents this afternoon. We all think it would be best if you stay at the church with me for a few days."

I jerk my shoulder from his clammy grasp without thinking. "I'm not going there with you." When I catch his horrified expression, I try softening the rejection with a grateful twitch of a smile. "Thank you for your generous offer, but I am fine staying at my own home."

"You call this fine?" His cassock-draped arms gesture to the meadow around us, to the forest lurking at my back. "No one is saying you would have to stay there indefinitely, but it will be good for you to clear your mind, and give you some time to spend with God, instead of out here tempting the Devil."

A million reasons tumble to my defense, but they all stop short.

Nothing I say will change his mind.

He and my parents have already decided, just as Cecily's had decided her future for her.

This is the way of the world we live in, where women like me are forced by the whims of the men who control them.

"You spoke to my father about this?"

He nods. "He is worried about you. We both are."

When he presses one of his hands to his chest, my stomach tightens. The compassion he's trying to convey in the gesture is sickening. He reeks of hunger and my bones quake at the thought of being devoured by the likes of him, let alone any man.

This is exactly what Doctor Egerton did with Catherine. What every powerful man has done with every woman before me.

Or maybe I am wrong. Maybe this is an entirely selfless act with no ulterior motives.

Unfortunately, I wouldn't know for certain until it is too late. And I cannot risk being right. I cannot risk living a life as the priest's plaything—as any man's plaything.

I cannot risk being caught and detained.

Before Father Thomas is any the wiser, I bolt for the shelter of the forest.

My name ricochets against the trees as he screams for me to come back to him. But I will not. I would rather plunge myself into the maw of death and be regurgitated back out again.

I would rather be taken by the Devil.

CHAPTER
FIVE

"Stop running from me, Ellowyn!"

Father Thomas' harsh voice crashes after me like a wild boar. He grunts and squeals every time he has to wedge himself between the narrow gaps in the trees that I slip through nimbly. And yet, he never falls too far behind. He's always right there, just barely out of reach.

"Come back with me now, before it's too late. I can keep you safe!"

He's panting now, as am I. But unlike him, I won't waste the breath it would take for me to explain to him that I have finally realized just how unsafe it is back home for me. I had no say in my future there. The only reason I survived as long as I did was because I followed the rules, kept a smile on my face, and kept every part of my true self hidden.

That's not safety.

That's a death sentence.

And I am ashamed it took me this long to recognize it.

Fear of ever returning to such an existence has carried me this far; it's pumped my legs with the adrenaline that's kept them running for what feels like hours. But my waterlogged skirts are beginning to weigh me down. It's like I'm trudging through a marsh of mud, and no matter how much I press onward, Father Thomas is faster yet.

The deeper we race into these woods, the more they feel like a maze that is slowly closing around me, entombing us both in its deadly clutches.

I don't know where I'm running. Where I hope to wind up. I just know I have to keep moving. I have to put distance between me and the life I almost allowed to swallow me.

Branches smack against the damp flesh of my cheeks like cracks of a horse whip, the sting of them like a jolt to my dying pace.

If I want to survive this, I have to lose Father Thomas.

But how?

At least a half dozen women have been taken into these woods, their bodies never found. I need to disappear like they have.

Another bough whacks me in the face, my teeth catching the brunt of its bite. The metallic zing of blood coats my tongue and I curse at the sun's dying light for not staying out a little longer. But it bids the sky a final farewell, and the forest descends into darkness.

I can't see more than a few inches in front of my face. And after colliding into a dozen or more elm trees, I'm forced to finally slow my gait.

Father Thomas calls my name again. His grating voice scrapes along my spine as if he's yelling it against my bare skin. However, it's clear from the frantic rising of frustration in his tone, and the way he seems to shout it in every direction, that he has no idea where I am.

The more he yells, the farther away he starts to sound.

In the chaos of the darkness, it seems I have finally lost him and found my advantage. Or perhaps the forest has finally claimed me. Veiled me the same way it has the others. Either way, it's not an opportunity I intend to squander.

Once I catch my breath, I ease into every step, careful not to snap any twigs on the forest floor. But I swear, it's like every leaf crunches and cracks like glass, and the dense canopy above me acts like the ceiling of a cave, making every noise reverberate and boom. Earlier I had thought maybe the forest was helping me. Now I'm not so sure. Perhaps this is the price I pay for entering the Devil's domain uninvited.

But I had been invited, hadn't I?

I saw the flash of red. That should've been invitation enough. It's all Cecily saw, anyway, so I should belong here just as much as she does.

As if the forest is mocking me, the second the thought crosses my mind, the moist dirt gives beneath my feet. Before I can catch myself, I'm falling—yelping as I slide down the ravine, the palms of my hands gliding over moss-covered logs and rocks until I land in a steady stream of ice-cold water. My breath hitches as the frigid water fills my boots and balloons my skirts.

On shaking legs, I wobble to my feet, desperate to get out of the cold, even though I'm starting to understand that there is no end in sight of that for me tonight. My garments have been soaked through since midday. If I stay out here much longer, I will likely catch cold—and that's only if I don't freeze to death first.

If there were ever a time to give up, it would be now. Surely, Father Thomas heard my fall; he will be here within a matter of moments, and I could take his hand and allow him to guide me back to town. I could submit to him, to my father, and lead the life they were laying out for me.

A different version of myself might have. But I don't know that woman anymore. And despite how this may end tonight, I am glad she's gone.

Since I can't turn back, I charge forward, braving the cold stream—nay, river—I have to cross.

The current is strong this time of year, the water deeper than I anticipate, but not so deep that I'm swimming through it. Even with my sodden skirts, I'm able to wade across without much trouble, only slipping on the slick rocks a handful of times, but that only means that Father Thomas will find ease with it as well.

Once I'm on the safety of the other side though, I realize I haven't heard him calling for me in some time. Not since before my fall.

The silence is thick and unnerving.

I almost prefer his hollering. At least then I knew where he was. Now, he can jump out at any moment. If it came down to a match of physical prowess, I have no doubt that even Father Thomas would be able to over-power me eventually, especially the way the chill is seeping into my bones.

But as I stand at attention, more alert and focused than I have ever been, I hear no hint of movement anywhere. No footsteps or panting. Only the river surges behind me, and even it is already muffled by the thick undergrowth surrounding it.

Perhaps Father Thomas gave up. Maybe he got lost and turned around.

A quiet, insidious voice in the back of my mind hopes that maybe the forest is protecting me, that whatever evil was lying dormant here has finally awak-ened with the fading sunlight and has ripped him away from me to keep me safe.

The thought puts me at ease, surprisingly, and soon I continue inward, embarking upon this new, unknown path with a renewed sense of assuredness.

The ascent up the other side of the ravine is still grueling; my boots are slick against the muddy earth and I slip numerous times, each fall earning me a new scrape or bruise that feels like a badge of honor. Each injury bolsters me. Maybe I'm not so fragile as I thought I was.

I keep climbing. Keep moving toward a future that I know nothing about, but one that I am sure will be better than what I could have ever faced back home.

Finally, I see the top of the hill.

On all fours, I climb to the summit.

A cool breeze wraps itself around me. It's the first time the air hasn't felt stagnated since I entered the tightly bound forest, and when I look up, I realize why. The canopy isn't suffocating the forest floor, but instead its been ripped open, allowing silver moonlight to cast the meadow before me in a shimmering, ethereal glow. Its beauty nearly steals my breath away, but its relief that lands the final blow. I made it. I finally outran the worst of my fate.

Or at least, that's what I think until I see the three figures standing as still as ghosts at the meadow's edge.

They're naked from the neck down, their breasts and pubic regions bared to the night as if in offering. Only their faces are hidden, each of them wearing a helm made from an animal skull. The two women on the sides seem to have wolf or coyote skulls, while the matriarch in the middle—a woman whose body is weathered and wrinkled in places that the others' aren't —is wearing a skull that is decidedly larger. A bear, perhaps—although, I didn't know bears dwelled in these woods.

Atop her head, she wears an ornate crown of antlers and foliage, and there is no mistaking that I have found the queen of the forest—the Devil *Her*self.

Compelled by the otherworldly moonlight and something else seemingly supernatural at play here, I bow before her.

When she speaks, she sounds nothing like the hideous demon I thought she would be.

"Why have you come here, child? We did not summon you." There is a weariness in her tone, a shaking rattle that sounds far too tired to be anything but human.

My brow scrunches with confusion, and I lift my head. "But...I saw the red eyes. I thought you were calling to me. I thought I'd been invited."

Ire jerks the matriarch's attention somewhere to the trees beside her, her bear skull and antlers clacking against one another from the sudden movement. I can only see as far as the moonlight will allow me, and the trees cast everything else in pitch-darkness, but I'm sure someone else is waiting there.

After a moment, the matriarch shifts her gaze back upon me and stands taller. "It would seem you have been called upon. So I'll ask you again, why have you come here?"

A test. One that I have no clue how to pass.

"I had no other choice!" I blurt out before I can think better of it.

The matriarch tsks, but she doesn't respond immediately. The bear's hollow eye sockets linger on me a moment, as she watches the chill of the night burrow into me until my teeth are rattling.

"Leave. Return to your home," she says, sounding displeased. "You are not ready. We do not accept you."

I think I hear someone gasp from the tree line, but my heart is thrumming too wildly to focus on it. *Return home?* I can't go back there. Not now. Not ever. When I fled tonight, it wasn't just on a whim, and I wasn't only fleeing a place. I was running from the ideals there. The traditions and beliefs that I have long-since outgrown. I no longer want them.

If I go back now, I'll never survive.

The matriarch turns around and begins hobbling away, with her two skull-faced friends doing the same.

"Wait!" I call out, desperation like a vise squeezing my throat. "I can't go back there. I—I don't belong there."

The matriarch and her disciples halt. They keep their bare backs turned toward me, but they're ready to hear my final plea.

I swallow hard. It's now or never, and I bare myself to them the way they are bared to me, leaving nothing unspoken. Nothing hidden.

"You asked me why I came here. I said I didn't have a choice, but I misspoke. I didn't mean I had no choice in coming here, what I meant was I couldn't stay where I was any longer. My home is not my home. The people there, they—they don't accept me. They want to conform me into something I'm not and..." My voice wavers when I think of Cecily. How many years I wasted trying to hide my love for her. "There was a woman. I loved her with every part of myself, and she loved me in return. They were going to take her away from me and I was going to allow it. Not anymore."

My eyes scan the tree line, understanding beginning to creep in.

At least a half dozen women have disappeared in these woods over the last year, and Edith was the first. I remember her raspy voice, the slow way with which she moved. But most of all, I remember how charismatic she was, how she was the center of attention in any room we ever shared. She was the kind of woman you sought out if you had nowhere else to go. She was the kind of woman I could easily see leading an army of others.

If Edith is here, if she has become the matriarch before me, and if all the other women who've gone missing are here, then so is—

"Cecily, if you're out there, I want you to know I came for you just as much as I came for myself." I pause long enough for her to respond, but when she doesn't, it's easy to let the words pour out. "I'm sorry. I was wrong not to leap at your request to leave it all behind. I see that now. I see how we both would've rotted in

Thimbleton, and I won't accept that existence any longer."

With fire in my eyes, I return my gaze to the matriarch. I swear something like pride is exuding from her black, hollow eyes.

"I came here because I am ready to lead a different life. I came because I am ready to live as I am, as I always have been."

Resolutely, the matriarch nods once, twice. With a flick of her wrinkled hand, she gestures to the tree line beside her. Two more women step forward, naked from foot to neck, aside from the skull masks that hide their faces.

I recognize one of them instantly.

I have spent many hours memorizing every curve of her voluptuous body. Every dimple in her thighs. Every crease in her belly. Every stretch mark and freckle and scar. I know Cecily by scent and sound, and even by other senses that I cannot put into words.

"Cecily!"

I start to run toward her but stop short when I realize she's holding onto something—someone.

She and her masked friend are dragging forth a man dressed in all black. His white collar is askew, his mouth gagged. But his wild eyes meet mine and I recognize him as well.

"Father Thomas?"

Edith and her disciples start to come forward. They beckon me forth as well and I shiver the entire way until we're all convened in the middle of the meadow, these not-so-missing women, myself, and their prisoner.

Edith holds out a hand and I set mine atop it, her skin cool and dry. I'm not expecting it when she flips my palm upward and places a bloodstained ritual knife inside it.

"What's this for?" I ask.

"A sacrifice must be made." She tilts her head to the moon. "Be quick. We will need to prepare him before sunrise."

"Prepare him?" I glance down at Father Thomas where he is whimpering on his knees. "You—you want me to kill him? But he's done nothing wrong."

One of the other masked figures scoffs. I don't recognize her as easily as I have Edith and Cecily, but when I notice the needle marks in the crooks of her elbows, I make an educated guess.

Catherine.

She had always been a small thing—as thin as straw, as folks would say. It makes the roundness of her belly all the more noticeable.

Edith silences her with a glare before asking me, "Do you truly believe that? Do you believe this man to be sincerely and wholly innocent?" Her pause is expectant, but I can't muster a response. My own uncomfortable memories with him only make the dagger heavier. "Let me ask you this then, child, how many people's lives has he ruined? How many women has he condemned—and led others to condemn as well—just for being true to themselves?"

The more she speaks, the more of my memories she raises from the dead. Like how Father Thomas has always been the first to tarnish a woman's name after a supposed scandal. When Edith disappeared all those months ago, it was he who proclaimed her to be ill-minded. When Catherine began to show signs of hallucination, it was Father Thomas who organized her stay with the doctor, ultimately setting her engagement in motion—and perhaps even her pregnancy.

And the instant I began to fall out of line, he had tried to do the same with me.

He did more than just meddle in people's lives, however. For years, I convinced myself I was making up all of his furtive glances, the unwanted grazes of his hand against my thigh or wrist. The way his hungry eyes would linger on Cecily's bosom—or any other supple young woman's, for that matter.

Before tonight, I didn't have proof that he was a dangerous man, only an insistent nagging that I felt unsafe in his presence.

How many others before me felt the same way?

How many others could I protect here tonight with one stroke of a blade?

Glancing from the sharp curve of the knife, I bring my gaze up to the woman I love. They found another man's body at the edge of the forest just a few days ago, sliced to ribbons like all the others. I hadn't remembered at the time, but Albert had been visiting then. He had come the minute he heard of Cecily's disappearance. Was he the price she paid for her freedom? If so, I can tell by the ease of her breaths, from the steady rise and fall of her bared chest that she does not regret it.

One by one, I assess the women before me.

For years, they played by their rules. They stuffed their bodies in corsets and crinoline. They practiced their manners, their demure smiles, and tittered at unwanted compliments. They took care of entire households, raised children, and were still told that they weren't enough. That they were weaker than men. More simple-minded. More hysterical and far more inferior in all ways.

My grip tightens around the knife.

None of them are innocent. Anyone who continues to live that charade is guilty by default, let alone the people in power who are actively perpetuating it.

If this is my ticket at freedom, at a new life, I will take it.

In one swift motion, I plunge the dagger into Father Thomas' neck.

As he lay bleeding out in in the middle of the meadow, my sisters help me shed my clothes and the last vestiges of my old life. For the first time ever, I am bared down to my soul, unapologetically myself.

Cecily fastens a skull to my face, one that matches hers. Then she takes my hand into hers, and me and my sisters dance in the moonlight like the feral creatures we were always destined to be.

Thank you for reading *The Devil in the Woods*!

Leave a Review
Help other readers find this witchy, spooky read by leaving a review on Amazon, Goodreads, Bookbub, or any other reading website. Even a simple "I loved it!" can really help!

Newsletter
Stay up to date on all my latest releases and join my newsletter: http://eepurl.com/ggIjiX

Social Media
And last but not least, if you'd like to stay connected, you can find my social media links here: https://linktr.ee/jessaca_with_an_a

REAPERS OF VELTUUR
YA Epic Dark Fantasy

One reaper girl, and her path to redemption...

Sinisa is a Reaper, an assassin born from the underrealm, with fatal magic coursing through their veins.

She only needs one more kill to ascend as a Shade, a coveted status of power. And when the King of Oakfall requests a Reaper to execute his daughter for an unforgivable crime, Sinisa is first to volunteer for the job.

It *should* be easy.

But the Prince discovers his father's plans, flees the palace with his sister, and Sinisa is left with no choice but to journey through the mortal realm to find and slay her mark.

No one can outrun a Reaper... Or can they?

Check out the Reapers of Veltuur Trilogy on Amazon

PRIMORDIALS OF SHADOWTHORN
Epic Dark Fantasy Romance

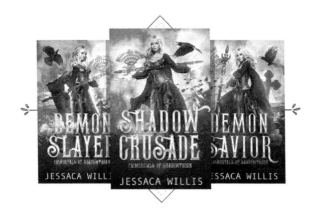

Ruled by tyrants. Hunted by demons.
This vengeful huntress is ready to fight back.

When Halira's parents are slaughtered by the horrifying demons that plague her lands, she joins the Shadow Crusade, a legion of warriors determined to slay the last living Primordial, end its reign of darkness, and destroy demon-kind once and for all.

But as her training begins, Halira soon discovers a secret about the forgotten magic that once thrived throughout the lands, one that could threaten her very survival.

Will Halira be the savior her country needs, or will her own dark secret force her to hide in the shadows?

Check out the Primordials of Shadowthorn series—the prelude to Blood & Magic Eternal—on Amazon

ABOUT THE AUTHOR

Jessaca is a fantasy writer with an inclination toward the dark, epic, and romantic sub-genres. She draws inspiration from books like Nevernight & ACOTAR, videogames like Dark Souls III, and television shows like Game of Thrones and The Witcher. She is a self-proclaimed nerd who loves cosplay, video games, and comics, and if you live in the PNW, you just might see her at one of the local comic conventions dressed in one of her favorite RWBY cosplays!

Printed in Great Britain
by Amazon